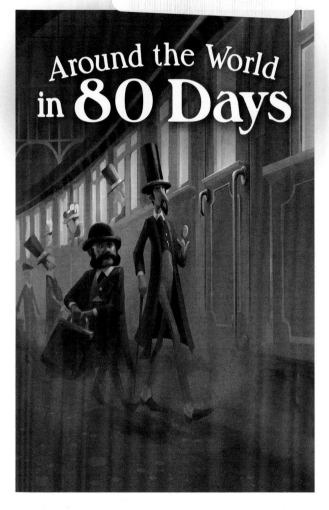

Around the World in 80 Days

Adapted by Dona Herweck Rice
Illustrated by Fernando Juarez

Publishing Credits

Rachelle Cracchiolo, M.S.Ed., *Publisher*
Conni Medina, M.A.Ed., *Editor in Chief*
Nika Fabienke, Ed.D., *Content Director*
Véronique Bos, *Creative Director*
Shaun N. Bernadou, *Art Director*
Noelle Cristea, M.A.Ed., *Senior Editor*
John Leach, *Assistant Editor*
Jess Johnson, *Graphic Designer*

Image Credits

Illustrated by Fernando Juarez. p.4 Félix Nadar.

Library of Congress Cataloging-in-Publication Data

Names: Rice, Dona, adapter. | Juarez, Fernando, illustrator. | Verne,
   Jules, 1828-1905. Tour du monde en quatre-vingts jours.
Title: Around the world in 80 days / adapted by Dona Herweck Rice ;
   illustrated by Fernando Juarez.
Other titles: Around the world in eighty days
Description: Huntington Beach, CA : Teacher Created Materials, [2020] |
   Includes book club questions. | Audience: Age 9. | Audience: Grades 4-6.
Identifiers: LCCN 2019034830 (print) | LCCN 2019034831 (ebook) | ISBN
   9781644913734 (paperback) | ISBN 9781644914632 (ebook)
Subjects: LCSH: Readers (Elementary) | Voyages around the world--Juvenile
   fiction.
Classification: LCC PE1119 .R46474 2020 (print) | LCC PE1119 (ebook) |
   DDC 428.6/2--dc23
LC record available at https://lccn.loc.gov/2019034830
LC ebook record available at https://lccn.loc.gov/2019034831

5301 Oceanus Drive
Huntington Beach, CA 92649-1030
www.tcmpub.com

ISBN 978-1-6449-1373-4

Table of Contents

Author's Note

Around the World in 80 Days, by Jules Verne, was published in 1873. Verne was inspired to write the story by the rapidly changing transportation methods around him. In Verne's lifetime, transportation evolved and travel became easier—though not as easy as it is today. Traveling around the world was a bold notion, and to circle the globe in 80 days was an outrageous thought. It would take an adventurer like Phileas Fogg to get the job done!

Verne's book is filled with twists and turns and plenty of detail. This highly abridged version focuses on just a few highlights of the nearly 24,000-mile journey in Verne's novel. It also alters some of the nineteenth-century perspectives on the British colonial lands that are apparent in the original.

CHAPTER ONE

◈

Race Against Time

Phileas Fogg, a wealthy English
gentleman and loner, spent his days like
clockwork. He woke, shaved, and ate
breakfast at the same time each day. He
spent afternoons at the Reform Club,
where he ate his lunch and dinner,
read his papers, and spent his evenings
playing the game whist with the same

group of other wealthy gentlemen. After whist, he went home, went to sleep, and woke to do it all again the next day. Fogg's manners were perfect and his habits predictable. Everyone knew exactly what to expect from Phileas Fogg.

Perhaps Fogg's lone servant, James Foster, should not have been surprised when he was immediately fired for the offense of providing shaving water that was two degrees too cold. Unforgivable! Fogg needed a new servant right away.

Enter Jean Passepartout (pass-par-TOO), a Frenchman with a wild past. He had been a fireman, a clown, a gymnast, and a singer. Now, he needed a new job. He hoped Fogg's quiet lifestyle and regular schedule would offer the calm his own life had been missing. Fogg thought Passepartout would suit him well and hired him on the spot. Passepartout got right to work.

But that very day, everything changed.

The gentlemen of the Reform Club enjoyed whist—in part because it was a game of bets and wagers. They appreciated a good gamble; therefore, they were thrilled when the opportunity to make an exciting bet arose.

"Have you heard about this abominable bank robbery?" a portly brewer named Flanagan began their conversation.

"I have, indeed. Do they know the identity of the robber?" asked a heavily mustachioed engineer named Stuart, glancing up from his cards and sipping his tea.

"It is no robber. It is a gentleman!" a gray-haired fellow by the name of Ralph added. He served as director of the very bank that had been robbed.

"He'll never get away with it!" Sullivan and Fallentin, both bankers, declared in unison.

"It's a big world," Ralph offered dejectedly. "He'll manage someplace to hide."

"Not so big as it once was," Fogg added matter-of-factly, setting aside the newspaper he'd been reading.

"Whatever do you mean, sir?" Ralph countered.

"The final section of railway between Rothal and Allahabad in India has been completed, or so the news reports," Fogg informed the group. "All the world is now easily connected, and by my calculations, the globe can be completely circumnavigated in just 80 days. That is a small world indeed. The gentleman will be discovered and delivered to justice in no time."

"Eighty days, you say?" spluttered Stuart, dribbling tea into his mustache.

"You may be correct in theory, Fogg," Flanagan challenged, "but in practical purposes, no one can travel the world in 80 days." The whist players chuckled at the absurdity of the notion, but Fogg's ears perked up. He heard a challenge!

"You think not, do you?" Fogg asked, eyes gleaming. "I wager it can be done;

11

in fact, I wager that I myself can do it!"

"A wager, you say?" Ralph asked. "I'll take that bet, and I offer £4,000 in my certainty you cannot do it."

"Ah, £4,000? Come, gentlemen. If you are men of conviction, the wager should easily be more money than that. Don't you agree? What about £20,000?"

The table fell silent—and then erupted in eager wage-making euphoria. "I'll take that bet!" "Count me in, Fogg!" "Harrumph! You're a fool, man. I'll gladly place odds against you."

"Gentlemen, gentlemen," Fogg silenced them all with a wave of his hand, "I accept." Then, he casually pulled his watch from his pocket, reading the time. "By this hour, 80 days from today, I will return to this very club, having traveled the circumference of the globe. I will place £20,000 on hold at the bank in good faith should I lose the wager. But believe me, gentlemen," Fogg's eyes gleamed, "I will not."

"We shall see," Ralph answered, and then asked, "But how will we verify that you have actually done this impossible task?"

"Nothing so simple, gentlemen. My passport will be stamped along the way, which should adequately prove my travels." Then, assuring that all matters of business were confirmed, Fogg added, "Shall we sign on it, gentlemen, and make it official?"

The men around the table quickly agreed, certain they would soon be sharing £20,000 among them.

"But Fogg, shouldn't you be on your way?" Flanagan asked.

"Not until we finish this game, my good fellow," Fogg casually replied, never having left a game unfinished and not inclined to do so now. And so, Fogg completed his hand—effortlessly beating the table and pocketing his winnings before excusing himself to begin his 80-day adventure.

CHAPTER TWO

◈

18 Days to Bombay

After winning his hand, Fogg raced home, surprising Passepartout with the haste in which he came through the door. "Pack a carpetbag, man!" Fogg shouted to Passepartout before taking the stairs two at a time to his dressing room to change for the journey. Fogg directed Passepartout to pack minimally, and the rest of what they needed would be purchased on the journey.

"Where are we going, monsieur?" Passepartout asked in confusion.

"Around the world, of course. Now pack, my good man. The train for Dover leaves in 10 minutes!" Fogg directed emphatically.

Passepartout stared openmouthed for a moment, and then, shaking his head, jumped into action. He knew Fogg was a strange man, but this was stranger than he could have imagined. However, Passepartout was loyal and dedicated when he gave his word, and so he decided to follow his new master on principle alone. He packed the basics, and away they went to begin their adventure.

The two made the Dover train just as the wheels on the track began to roll. They seated themselves, comfortable in a British railcar for the first leg of their journey. Fogg lost himself in his newspaper. Passepartout stared out a window and pondered just what he had gotten himself into.

"Surely, we will give up this madness and return home *tout de suite*," he whispered to his reflection in the window. The idea comforted him. He dozed while Fogg read and the train wheels clacked beneath them.

Fogg and Passepartout traveled all through Europe quite easily in this manner. Train to train, they whisked through France and Italy in just three days. At every stop, Passepartout was certain they would return home. But Fogg was calm and focused on the journey. He kept to himself unless he could find whist partners. Each night, he carefully entered data in his travel journal.

In Italy, the two boarded the steamship *Mongolia*. On it, they would journey to Egypt, Yemen, and finally Bombay, India. Fogg managed to convince the steamer captain to speed up their trip. A hefty reward made all the difference. The ship passed through Yemen with ease and arrived in Bombay two days early! Fogg was certain he'd win his bet.

Modern travel was a wonder! Until now, most travel in India was done by foot, horseback, or carriage. Rail and ship changed the game, making for quick and easy transport. Fogg was ready to make light work of crossing the country with the modern railway system.

The *Mongolia* docked in Bombay at four o'clock in the afternoon. Fogg and Passepartout had exactly four hours until boarding the train for Calcutta.

"We need more shirts and shoes, Passepartout," Fogg told his servant. "Use this time to get what we need, but return before the train departs. It will leave with or without you!"

"*Oui, monsieur.* I will make haste," Passepartout agreed, thinking to himself that he'd use some of the time

to see this intriguing city. Already, the sights and smells were calling him, and he was eager to answer. "Fogg has no interest in seeing the world—just traveling around it," Passepartout said aloud to himself as he walked into the city. "If I'm to see it, I must do so alone."

Passepartout quickly found the clothing he needed. As a result, he had a little spare time to look around. *What could be the harm in that?* he wondered. The sound of muffled cheers caught his attention. Turning a narrow street corner, a splash of color and music swept him up. He had wandered into a festival of some kind, just then spilling into the streets. Women in flowing scarves and glittering bangles danced snake-like all around him. He was mesmerized by their movements and their clanging tambourines. As they bent and twirled along the way, Passepartout followed, openmouthed and wide-eyed.

It took Passepartout a few minutes to notice he'd gone much farther than he had planned. But he was soon delighted that he did. He noticed an interesting Hindu temple in front of him. He had been hoping to see a temple! With the curiosity of a tourist, he decided to step inside and look around.

Passepartout had no idea that visitors to such temples must remove their shoes and hats before entering. It was law. On top of that, only Hindus were allowed inside. The government supported the religious practices of its people, and offenders would be punished. Passepartout was ignorant of his offense. It was clear that this brawny Frenchman in his English suit did not belong in the temple.

CHAPTER THREE

◈

Traveling Trunk

No sooner had Passepartout stepped inside than he found himself pinned to the flagstone floor. Three priests had knocked him down and were wrestling his shoes from his feet and the hat from his head. Fortunately for him, he had trained as an acrobat and was able to twist and snake from their clutches.

He ran from the temple with one of the priests at his heels; he dodged and darted amid the festival dancers. Finally losing his pursuer in the crowd, he sprinted for the depot.

Panting, Passepartout arrived at the station. He was disheveled and shoeless, but he had made it with five minutes to spare. He breathlessly boarded the train and slipped into the seat next to Fogg, who was calmly reading his newspaper as usual. In Fogg's mind, everything was running like clockwork.

Nearly three weeks into the adventure, a new thought dawned on Passepartout: Fogg really *did* intend to complete this journey. He had assumed all along that they would give up at any moment. But no—it was clear they were in it to the end.

"If Monsieur Fogg is committed to this wager, then he has my support, no matter what," Passepartout declared aloud. Suddenly realizing he was not alone, he looked around to find a fellow passenger staring at him quizzically. The Frenchman shrugged his shoulders and returned a sheepish smile.

The train journey across India began uneventfully, just as in Europe. Modern technology had created a rail system as dependable as the one they'd traveled before. Fogg read his papers, played whist when he could, and otherwise kept to his cabin. Passepartout watched out the windows, hoping to see something of the world they traveled. The train clacked, and the clock ticked. They were ahead of schedule.

"Monsieur Fogg, I believe you will win your bet!" Passepartout happily proclaimed to Fogg when pouring his morning tea.

"Most assuredly," Fogg responded, reaching for the cup, which shook violently in his hand as the train came to a sudden and dramatic stop.

"*Mon dieu!*" Passepartout cried.

Fogg calmly wiped the tea from his hand, stood up, and stepped to the doorway. Spotting the conductor outside the train, Fogg asked, "What is the meaning of this, my good man?"

"It's the end of the line, of course," the conductor answered.

"This train stops in Calcutta," Fogg replied. "We are decidedly not in Calcutta."

"Calcutta? Certainly not. The tracks have yet to be laid through to Allahabad. All passengers must make their own way from here until the tracks are set."

If Fogg was troubled by this news, he didn't show it beyond a raised eyebrow. He immediately got to work planning an alternative route to rejoin the train. He didn't notice his servant step away to approach a man in the distance. Passepartout returned with the man—and an elephant—a short while later.

"Monsieur Fogg, I have found your

answer!" Passepartout beamed. They
could ride the elephant the 50 miles
to Allahabad. Fogg was delighted,
patting Passepartout on the back. The
elephant's owner sold her to Fogg for
an enormous price, which Fogg paid
without blinking.

But one problem remained. They
had no idea how to ride an elephant.

"Monsieur, I think I know what to
do." Passepartout came to the rescue

once more. He found a guide who agreed to lead them to Allahabad. Fogg rode in a *howdah* basket with Passepartout. The guide perched on the elephant's neck.

The group headed into the forest, taking a shortcut that would shave 20 miles off their journey. The path was rough, and the elephant's tramping jostled the travelers. But after many hours of bumps, bruises, and jarred teeth (and a night of rest in an abandoned hut), the travelers reached Allahabad ahead of schedule!

"Thank you, my good man," Fogg said to the guide. Ever generous, he offered him the elephant.

"You have forever changed my life for the better!" the poor man cried, bowing in gratitude to Fogg.

"You are entirely welcome, sir," Fogg declared before turning to board the Calcutta train. They traveled on, ahead of schedule and more determined than ever to win the bet.

CHAPTER FOUR

❖

Out of Time

Twists and turns followed Fogg and Passepartout at every step of the journey. They rescued an Indian princess from certain death and offered her passage to England. They eluded prison in Calcutta, where they were arrested for violating the temple in Bombay. A hefty bail paid and a quick departure on a ship to Hong Kong saved them from that peril. From there, Fogg and the princess boarded a ship to Japan, but Passepartout was drugged and stranded. He made his own way, where he joined a circus for money—and Fogg found him.

Onward they traveled, across the seas to San Francisco and across the United States by train and a prairie sledge—a land boat of sorts that was moved by strong prairie winds. Fogg dueled, battled attackers on the train, and rescued Passepartout from kidnapping. From coast to coast they traveled, catching a last-minute ship from New York to France. Fogg bribed the ship's crew to mutiny and take him to England instead. It worked, and they reached England with six hours to spare! But stepping onto British soil, Fogg was arrested and thrown in jail.

Unknown to Fogg, he had been followed all the way by a detective from Scotland Yard. He believed Fogg was the bank robber! Who else would have so much cash to throw around? But after a few hours in jail, it was discovered that the true robber had already been arrested, and Fogg was released. Ever hopeful, he continued the journey, racing against the clock.

But there had been too many delays, and Fogg was too late. He was certain that he had lost the bet!

For the first time, Fogg lost his composure. He was now poor *and* a failure. However, the Indian princess loved him and asked him to marry her. He realized he loved her too. Then, Passepartout realized what none of them had. Traveling eastward, they had crossed time zones and were actually a day earlier than they thought!

Fogg raced to the Reform Club in the nick of time—and he won! He had traveled around the world in 80 days, and just like that, his well-ordered world was running like clockwork once again.

About Us

The Author

Dona Herweck Rice is the author of hundreds of books for children. She loves writing—and she loves reading even more. In fact, in her perfect world, she could open the cover of a book and step right inside it, having tea with Alice, learning magic with Harry, or traveling by cyclone with Dorothy. If you happen to read a book with a tall, curly-haired woman who doesn't seem to make sense in the story, you'll know she got her wish.

The Illustrator

Fernando Juarez is from Madrid, Spain, where he works as an illustrator and an art supervisor at an animation studio. He studied graphic design and illustration. He has three kids, and if he has any time left after work and family, you might catch him playing guitar in a rock band.

cipios encontrados en Proverbios 19:2, Efe-
nses 4:5. ¿Qué le dicen estos principios sobre
más importante?

os conforme al corazón de Dios

nismo a planear lo que resta del día de hoy.
erario esos eventos que ya están señalados,
ponsabilidades. Si está leyendo este libro de
planificar el día de mañana.

tiempo orando por sus prioridades. Si tiene una
a cada persona y responsabilidad. Si es una
con diligencia por los hijos. Si no está casada
hable con Dios sobre su lugar de trabajo, su
milia y sus amistades. Pídale a Dios que le dé
s de hacer su voluntad en cada categoría.

por la oración se gana más información, ore
as actividades de mañana.

emano cómo va a poner en práctica sus priori-
día. ¿Qué actividades o placeres podará para
os? ¿Qué va a hacer para adiestrar su corazón y
ir con su plan? Planifique de antemano cómo
pulsos y tentaciones que surjan en su camino.

ón que tiene para su vida? ¿Para su familia?
Entregue estos deseos de su corazón a Dios y
nudo, ¡para que Él y usted puedan trabajar
rlos!

---

habrán de edificarle. ¡Pídale a Dios que le dirija a medida que
usted enriquece su alma y espíritu!

Capítulo 19 - *Un corazón que muestra compasión*

- Tome un minuto para considerar su vida escondida. Medite en
  Colosenses 3:1-3. ¿Qué cambios diarios, sencillos o significati-
  vos, de estilo de vida haría para poder pasar más tiempo siendo
  llena de la bondad de Dios?

- ¿Cómo se califica a usted misma en cuanto a alcanzar a otros?
  ¿En cuanto a cuidar? ¿Se considera una persona dadivosa, o
  tacaña? Lea Proverbios 3:27. ¿Qué bienes está almacenando para
  los demás? Defina un plan claro de acción para abrir su mano y
  hacer el bien, y haga de esto un importante proceso de aprendi-
  zaje, un asunto de oración.

- ¿Qué hará exactamente para "dar" la próxima vez que vaya al
  servicio de adoración o a una actividad de la iglesia? Planifique
  con anticipación cada ocasión, para que pueda tener ese compor-
  tamiento como parte de su estilo de vida.

- ¡Regresamos a la oración! Lea Efesios 6:18. ¿Cree que la oración
  es un ministerio para los demás? ¿Por qué o por qué no? ¿Cuándo
  fue bendecida por un ministerio de oración? ¿Cuándo sirvió a
  Dios y a su pueblo por medio del ministerio de oración? Ahora
  escriba su tiempo, lugar y plan para orar. Antes que cierre este
  libro, pase un momento orando con todo su corazón, y compro-
  métase a seguir su plan de oración mañana.

Capítulo 20 - *Un corazón que anima*

- ¿Cuál consideraría que es una debilidad primordial en su vida, que le estorba cuando se trata de ministrar a los demás? Ya vimos la historia de dos mujeres que sufrieron de timidez. ¿De qué sufre usted que contribuye

- fracasa al ministrar a los demás? Menciónelo y luego enumere los pasos que puede dar esta semana para fortalecer esta debilidad y seguir adelante, venciéndola por completo. Cree un plan de acción.

- Califíquese en el área de memorizar Escrituras: *¿Con frecuencia, a menudo, por lo general, en ocasiones, o nunca* pone su mente a trabajar guardando la Palabra de Dios en su corazón? Lea y considere el Salmo 119:11.

- ¿Qué le impide memorizar las Escrituras? ¿Qué le ayudaría a memorizarlas? ¿Una compañera a quien rendir cuentas? ¿Seleccionar cinco versos para memorizar? ¿Apartar a diario el tiempo para memorizar? ¿Decidirse a memorizar mientras hace alguna otra cosa (planchar, caminar, manejar, sembrar, limpiar)? ¡Sea lo que sea que le motiva y ayuda, planéelo y póngalo en acción!

- Lea Isaías 50:4, Efesios 4:29, y Colosenses 4:6, y fíjese el ministerio que sus palabras pueden lograr. ¿Quién necesita una llamada, o nota de ánimo de usted? Haga esa llamada y escriba esa nota hoy.

- Lea nuevamente la descripción del ministerio de la mujer de Proverbios 31. He aquí alguien que dominó sus prioridades y las vivió para nosotras por toda la eternidad. ¿Qué aprende usted de

---

ella? ¿Cón
una mujer
beneficiars

Capítulo 21 -

- ¿Qué muest
hacer", sus
etc., sobre s
la realidad d
oración con
prioridades d
sus oraciones

- ¿Qué decision
nen sus priori
le ayudarían a
decisiones le g

- Enumere las pe
la lista de los s
de orar y leer la
nes en el orden
mente, haga una
en su libreta de
ore!

- Piense en la ver
esperar? Recuerd
la que no, y rec
esperar sea algo
Biblia pudieran a
Señor?

- Considere los pri
sios 5:15, y Colos
el poner primero

Capítulo 22 - *Ande*

- Comience ahora
Escriba en su iti
comidas, citas, re
noche, comience

- Ahora pase algún
familia, consider
madre soltera, or
en este momento
universidad, su
formas específic

- Confiando en q
por cada una de

- Determine de a
dades por sólo
servir mejor a D
mente para seg
enfrentará los i

- ¿Cuál es la vis
¿Para su hogar
revíselos a m
juntos y cump

Notas

Una palabra de bienvenida

1. Richard Foster, "And We Can Live By It: Discipline", *Decision Magazine,* septiembre 1982, p.11.
2. Ibid.

Capítulo Uno

1. Ray y Anne Ortlund, *The Best Half of Life* (Glendale, CA: Regal Books, 1976), p. 88.
2. Carole Mayhall, *From the Heart of a Woman* (Colorado Springs: NavPress, 1976), pp. 10-11.
3. Oswald J. Smith, *The Man God Uses* (London: Marshall, Morgan & Scott, 1925), pp. 52-57.
4. Andrew Murray, señalador.
5. Ray y Anne Ortlund, *The Best Half of Life,* pp. 24-25.
6. Betty Scott Stam, fuente desconocida.

Capítulo dos

1. Ray y Anne Ortlund, (The Best Half of Life (Glendale, CA: Regal Books, 1976), p. 79.
2. C.A. Stoddards, fuente desconocida.
3. Henry Drummond, *The Greatest Thing in the World* (Old Tappan, NJ: Compañía Fleming H. Revell, 1977), p. 42.
4. Jim Downing, *Meditation, The Bible Tells You How* (Colorado Springs: NavPress, 1976), pp. 15-16.
5. Robert D. Foster, *The Navigator* (Colorado Springs: NavPress, 1983), pp. 110-11.
6. J.C. Pollock, *Hudson Taylor and Maria* (Grand Rapids, MI: Zondervan Publishing House, 1975), p. 169.
7. J.C. Pollock, *Hudson Taylor and Maria,* p. 169
8. Anne Ortlund, *The Disciplines of the Beautiful Woman* (Waco, TX: Word, Incorporated, 1977), p. 103.

9. Mrs. Charles E. Cowman, *Streams in the Desert*, Vol. 1 (Grand Rapids, MI: Zondervan Publishing House, 1965), p. 330.

10. Robert D. Foster, *The Navigator*, pp. 64-65.

11. *Los Angeles Times*, obituario de William Schuman, febrero 17, 1992.

Capítulo tres

1. Corrie Ten Boom, *Don't Wrestle, Just Nestle* (Old Tappan, NJ: Revell, 1978), p. 79.

2. Oswald Chambers, *Christian Disciplines* (Grand Rapids, MI: Discovery House Publishers, 1995), p. 117.

3. James Dobson, *What Wives Wish Their Husbands Knew About Women* (Wheaton, IL: Tyndale House Publishers, Inc., 1977), p. 22.

4. Edith Schaeffer, *Common Sense Christian Living* (Nashville: Thomas Nelson Publishers, 1983), pp. 212-15.

5. Edith Schaeffer, *Common Sense Christian Living*, pp. 212-15.

Capítulo cuatro

1. Curtis Vaughan, ed., *The Old Testament Books of Poetry from 26 Translations* (Grand Rapids, MI: Zondervan Bibles Publishers, 1973), pp. 478-79

2. Curtis Vaughan, ed., *The Old Testament Books of Poetry from 26 Translations, p. 277.*

Capítulo cinco

1. Charles F. Pfeiffer y Everett F. Harrison, eds., *The Wycliffe Bible Commentary* (Chicago: Moody Press, 1973), p. 5.

2. Ray y Anne Ortlund, *The Best Half of Life* (Glendale, CA: Regal Books, 1976), p. 97.

3. Julie Nixon Eisenhower, *Special People* (New York: Ballantine Books, 177), p. 199.

4. Julie Nixon Eisenhower, *Special People* , p. 80.

Capítulo seis

1. W. E. Vine, *An Expository Dictionary of New Testament Words* (Old Tappan, NJ: Fleming H. Revell Company, 1966), p. 86.

2. *Webster's New Collegiate Dictionary* (Springfield, MA: G. & C. Merriam Co., Publishers, 1961), p. 845.

3. Elisabeth Elliot, *The Shaping of a Christian Family* (Nashville: Thomas Nelson Publishers, 1992), p. 75.

4. Curtis Vaughan, ed., *The New Testament from 26 Translations* (Grand Rapids, MI: Zondervan Publishing House, 1967), p. 888.

5. Sheldon Vanauken, *Under the Mercy* (San Francisco: Ignatius Pres, 1985), pp. 194-95.

Capítulo siete

1. Gene Getz, *The Measure of a Woman* (Glendale, CA: Gospel Light Publications, 1977), pp. 75-76.

2. Jill Briscoe, *Space to Breathe, Room to Grow* (Wheaton, IL: Victor Books, 1985), pp. 184-187.

3. Anne Ortlund, *Building a Great Marriage* (Old Tappan, NJ: Fleming H. Revell Company, 1984), p. 146.

4. Anne Ortlund, *Building a Great Marriage* citando a Howard y Charlotte Clinebell, p. 170.

5. Charlie Shedd, *Talk to Me* (Old Tappan, NJ: Fleming H. Revell Company, 1976), pp. 65-66.

6. Curtus Vaughan, ed., *The Old Testament Books of Poetry from 26 Translations* (Grand Rapids, MI: Zondervan Bibles Publishers, 1973), p. 572.

Capítulo ocho

1. Edith Schaeffer, *What Is a Family?* (Old Tappan, NJ: Fleming H. Revell Company, 1975), p. 87.

2. Jack y Carole Mayhall, *Marriage Takes More Than Love* (Colorado Springs: NavPress, 1978), p. 154. Citando Kay K. Arvin, *One Plus One Equals One* (Nashville: Broadman Press, 1969), pp. 37-38.

3. Anne Ortlund, *Building a Great Marriage* (Old Tappan, NJ: Fleming H. Revell Company, 1984), p. 157.

4. Julie Nixon Eisenhower, *Special People* (Nueva York: Ballantine Books, 1977), pp. 52-53.

5. Betty Frist, *My Neighbors, The Billy Grahams* (Nashville: Broadman Press, 1983), p. 31.

6. William MacDonald, *Enjoying the Proverbs* (Kansas City, KS: Walterick Publishers, 1982), p. 56.

Capítulo nueve

1. Phil Whisenhunt, *Good News Broadcaster,* mayo 1971, p. 20.

2. Stanley High, *Billy Graham* (Nueva York: McGraw Hill, 1956), p. 28.

3. Abigail Van Buren, *Dear Abby, Los Angeles Times,* fecha desconocida.

4. Stanley High, *Billy Graham,* p. 126.

5. Carole C. Carlson, *Corrie Ten Boom: Her Life, Her Faith* (Old Tappan, NJ: F. H. Revell Co., 1983), p. 33.

6. Elisabeth Elliot, *The Shaping of a Christian Family* (Nashville: Thomas Nelson Publishers, 1992), p. 58.

7. Sra. Howard Taylor, *John and Betty Stam: A Story of Triumph,* edición revisada (Chicago: Moody Press, 1982), p. 15.

8. Elisabeth Elliot, *The Shaping of a Christian Family,* pp. 205-06.

Capítulo diez

1. H. D. M. Spence y Joseph S. Exell, eds., *The Pulpit Commentary, Volumen 9* (Grand Rapids, MI: Wm. B. Eerdmans Publishing Company, 1978), p. 595.

2. Charles Bridges, *A Modern Study in the Book of Proverbs,* revisado por George F. Santa (Milford, MI: Mott Media, 1978), p. 728.

3. H.D.M. Spence y Joseph S. Exell, eds., *The Pulpit Commentary, Volumen 9,* p. 607.

4. Stanley High, *Billy Graham* (Nueva York: McGwaw Hill, 1956), p. 71.

5. Linda Raney Wright, *Raising Children* (Wheaton, IL: Tyndale House Publishers, Inc., 1975), p. 50.

6. E. Schuyler English, *Ordained of the Lord* (Neptune, NJ: Loizeaux Brothers, 1976), p. 35.

7. Marilee Pierce Dunker, *Man of Vision: Woman of Prayer* (Nashville: Thomas Nelson Publishers, 1980), p. 166.

Capítulo once

1. Marvin R. Vincent, *Word Studies in the New Testament,* Vol. IV (Grand Rapids, MI: Wm. B. Eerdmans, Publishing Co., 1973), p. 341.

2. Dwight Spotts, "What is Child Abuse?" in *Parents & Teenagers,* Jay Kesler, ed. (Wheaton, IL: Victor Books, 1984), p. 426.

3. Curtis Vaughan, ed., *The Old Testament Books of Poetry from 26 Translations* (Grand Rapids, MI: Zondervan bible Publishers, 1973), p. 399.

4. Gary Smalley, *For Better or for Best* (Grand Rapids, MI: Zondervan Publishing House, 1988), p. 95.

5. Edith Schaeffer, *What Is a Family?* (Old Tappan, NJ: Fleming H. Revell Company, 1975).

6. Abigail Van Buren, *Dear Abby, Los Angeles Times,* fecha desconocida.

Capítulo doce

1. Julie Nixon Eisenhower, *Special People* (Nueva York: Ballantine Books, 1977), p. 69.

2. Linda Dillow, *Creative Counterpart* (Nashville: Thomas Nelson Publishers, 1977), p. 24.

Capítulo trece

1. Catherine Marshall, *A Man Called Peter* (Nueva York: McGraw-Hill, 1961), p. 65.

2. James Strong, *Strong's Exhaustive Concordance of the Bible* (Nashville: Abingdon Press, 1973), p. 22.

3. Robert Alden, *Proverbs* (Grand Rapids, MI: Baker Book House, 1983), p. 110.

4. Edith Schaeffer, *What Is a Family?* (Old Tappan, NJ: Fleming H. Revell Company, 1975).

5. Julie Nixon Eisenhower, *Special People* (Nueva York: Ballantine Books, 1977), p. 209.

6. Jim Conway, *Men in Mid-Life Crisis* (Elgin, IL: David C. Cook Publishing Company, 1987), pp. 250-52.

7. Edith Schaeffer, *Tapestry* (Waco, TX: Word Books, 1981), p. 616.

8. James strong, *Strong's Exhaustive Concordance of the Bible,* p. 34.

9. William J. Peterson, *Martin Luther Had a Wife* (Wheaton, IL: Tyndale House Publishers, Inc., 1983), p. 67.

10. Bonnie McCullough, *Los Angeles Times,* fecha desconocida.

Capítulo catorce

1. Jo Berry, *The Happy Home Handbook* (Old Tappan, NJ: Fleming H. Revell Co., 1976), pp. 41-56.

2. James Strong, *Strong's Exhaustive Concordance of the Biblia* (Nashville: Abingdon Press, 1973), p. 118.

3. H. D. M. Spence y Joseph S. Exell, *Pulpit Commentary, Vol. 8* (Grand Rapids, MI: Wm. B. Eerdmans Publishing Company, 1978), p. 30.

4. Derek Kidner, *Psalm 1-72* (Downers Gove, IL: InterVarsity Press, 1973), p. 48.

5. William Peterson, *Martin Luther Had a Wife* (Wheaton, IL: Tyndale House Publishers, Inc., 1983), p. 81.

Capítulo quince

1. Curtis Vaughan, ed., *The New Testament from 26 Translations* (Grand Rapids, MI: Zondervan Publishing House, 1967), p. 981.

2. James Strong, *Strong's Exhaustive Concordance of the Bible* (Nashville: Abingdon Press, 1973), p. 51.

3. William Peterson, *Martin Luther Had a Wife* (Wheaton, IL: Tyndale House Publishers, Inc., 1983), p. 27.

4. Alan Lakein, *How to Control Your Time and Your Life* (Nueva York: Signet Books, 1974), p. 48.

Capítulo dieciséis

1. H. D.M. Spence y Joseph S. Exell, *Pulpit Commentary, Vol. 21* (Grand Rapids, MI: Casa Publicadora Wm. B. Eerdmans, 1978), p. 36.

2. James Strong, *Strong's Exhaustive Concordance of the Bible* (Nashville: Abingdon Press, 1973), p. 51.

3. Donald Guthrie, *Tyndale New Testament Commentaries, The Pastoral Epistles* (Grand Rapids, MI: Wm. B. Eerdmans Publishing House, 1976), p. 194.

4. Robert Jamieson, A. R. Fausset, y David Brown, *Commentary on the Whole Bible* (Grand Rapids, MI: Zondervan Publishing House, 1973), p. 1387.

5. Curtis Vaughan, ed., *The New Testament from 26 Translations* (Grand Rapids, MI: Zondervan Publishing House, 1967), p. 1017.

6. Anne Ortlund, *Love Me with Tough Love* (Waco, TX: Word, Incorporated, 1979), página desconcida.

Capítulo diecisiete

1. Ted. W. Engstrom, *The Pursuit of Excellence* (Grand Rapids, MI: Zondervan Publishing House, 1982), pp. 30-31.

2. Anne Ortlund, *The Disciplines of the Beautiful Woman* (Waco, Tx: Word, Incorporated, 1977), pp. 96,98.

Capítulo dieciocho

1. Moody Correspondence School, 820 North LaSalle Street, Chicago, IL 60610, 1-800-621-7105.

2. Jim George, *Friendship Evangelism* (Christian Development Ministries, P O Box 33166, Granada Hills, CA 91344, 1-800-542-4611), 1984.

3. *Discipleship Evangelism* (Grace Bookdshack, 13248 Roscoe Boulevard, Sun Valley, CA 91352, 1-800-472-2315).

4. Elizabeth George, *Learning to Lead: Ministry Skills for Women* (Christian Development Ministries, P O Box 33166, Granada Hills, CA 91344, 1-800-542-4611), 1991.

5. Elizabeth George, *Loving God with All Your Mind* (1994) y *God's Garden of Grace: Growing in the Fruit of the Spirit* (1995) (Eugene, OR: Harvest House Publishers).

6. Jack y Carole Mayhall, *Marriage Takes More Than Love* (Colorado Springs: NavPress, 1978), p. 157.

7. Betty Frist *My Neighbors, The Billy Grahams* (Nashville: Broadman Press, 1983), 143.

8. Michael LeBoeuf, *Working Smart* (Nueva York: Warner Books, 1979), p. 182.

9. Ted W. Engstrom, *The Pursuit of Excellence* (Grand Rapids, MI: Zondervan Publishing House, 1982), página desconocida.

10. Michael LeBoeuf, *Working Smart,* p. 182.

11. Denis Waitley, *Seeds of Greatness* (Old Tappan, NJ: Flemingt H. Revell Co. 1983), p. 95.

12. Gigi Tchividjian, *In Search of Serenity* (Portland, OR: Multnomah, 1990), página desconocida.

Capítulo diecinueve

1. Elisabeth Elliot, *Through Gates of Splendor* (Old Tappan, NJ: Fleming H. Revell Co., 1957), página desconocida.
2. Anne Ortlund, *The Disciplines of the Beautiful Woman* (Waco, TX: Word, Inc. , 1977), p. 35.
3. J. Sidlow Baxter, "Will and Emotions," *Alliance Life Magazine* (antes *Alliance Witness*), noviembre 1970. Usado con permiso.
4. Elizabeth George, *Woman of Excellence* (Christian Development Ministries, P. O. Box 33166, Granada Hills CA 91394, 1-800-542-4611), 1987.

Capítulo veinte

1. Charles Caldwell Ryrie, *Balancing the Christian Life* , (Chicago: Moody Press, 1969), pp. 96-97.
2. Charles Caldwell Ryrie, *Balancing the Christian Life*, pp. 96-97.
3. C. A. Stoddards, fuente desconocida.

Capítulo veintiuno

1. Janice Ericson. Usado con permiso del autor.
2. Michael DeBoeuf, *Working Smart* (Nueva York: Warner Books, 1979), pp. 129, 249.
3. *The Amplified Bible* (Grand Rapids , MI: Zondervan Bible Publishers, 1965), p. 302).
4. Pat King, *How Do You Find the Time?* (Edmonds, WA: Aglow Publications, 1975), página desconocida.
5. Pat King, *How Do You Find the Time?*, página desconocida.

Capítulo veintidós

1. Curtis Vaughan, ed., *The Old Testament Books of Poetry from 26 Translations* (Grand Rapids, MI: Zondervan Bible Publishing, 1973), p. 276.